THE DAY
THE EARTH
ROSE UP

Written and Illustrated by
ALFREDA BEARTRACK-ALGEO

7th Generation
Summertown, Tennessee

Library of Congress Cataloging-in-Publication Data available upon request.

We chose to print this title on paper certified by The Forest Steward-ship Council® (FSC®), a global, not-for-profit organization dedicated to the promotion of responsible forest management worldwide.

Printed in China

7th Generation
Book Publishing Company
PO Box 99, Summertown, TN 38483
888-260-8458
bookpubco.com
nativevoicesbooks.com

ISBN: 978-1-939053-39-8

27 26 25 24 23 22   1 2 3 4 5 6 7 8 9

Dedication

This book is dedicated to my grandchildren: Melana, Daniel, Harley, Peggy, Elizabeth, and Duwayne Jr., as well as many other hunka grandchildren. May you always believe in your dreams.

To my husband, David, for your constant love and support. To my friends, for always giving me encouragement just when I need it most. To my family, especially my beloved parents, for being my source of strength and inspiration. And, most humbly, to my Lakota elders, for keeping our traditions alive and well.

Author's Note

The legend of the Pleiades has fascinated humanity since the beginning of time. As a child, I was told stories of the Pleiades as well, like the story of Hinhan Kaga Paha and the constellation Wicincala Sakowin (the Seven Sisters). Through the years, I have dreamed and heard many stories of the Pleiades. These stories often share similar concepts and metaphors with the one I heard growing up. Many of these stories depict humans interacting equally with the heavenly bodies, the elements, the animal nations, the water nations, the plant nations, and the stone spirits.

The Day the Earth Rose Up is a story that depicts my personal view of the sacred relationship between the Paha Sapa (Black Hills), the Mato Tipila (Bear Lodge), the Mato Paha (Bear Mountain), and the Wicincala Sakowin (Seven Sisters), and shows how everyone and everything is interconnected. What is sacred above, is sacred below. Mitakuye Oyasin: we are all related.

I add my story to the many other stories within our oral traditions and sacred narratives that keep us immersed in our histories. It is my hope that *The Day the Earth Rose Up* will connect readers to this sacred concept.

Glossary of Lakota Words

Até: father

Hanhepi: night sky

Hanwi: moon

Hinhan Kaga Paha: Black Elk Peak, the highest peak in the Black Hills of South Dakota

Iná: mother

Kul Wicasa Oyate: Lower Brule Lakota People

Mahpiya: Sky World

Maka: Earth World

Mato Paha: Bear Mountain

Mato Sica: Giant Bear

Mato Tipila: Bear Lodge

Mitakuye Oyasin: we are all related

Paha Sapa: Black Hills in South Dakota and Wyoming

Tinpsila: wild turnips

Tipi: lodge dwelling

Tiyóspaye: family

Wanbli Tanka: GreatEagle

Wakan Tanka: Great Spirit

Waziya: north, or the old man of the north

Wi: sun

Wicahpi: Star Nation

Wicincala Sakowin: Seven Sisters (or Pleiades constellation)

Wojapi: chokecherry pudding

ong ago in Maka (Earth World), a young girl named Maske lived with her tiyóspaye (family) in a village at the edge of the Paha Sapa (Black Hills). The village had many lodges, called tipis, arranged in a circle facing east. Maske's tipi was on the south side of the village. Maske's Até (father) painted the outside of their tipi with running buffalo and deer, colorful symbols of his achievements. Maske's Iná (mother) kept their tipi warm and safe and filled with many soft buffalo skins. She made Maske and her sisters beautiful porcupine-quill moccasins and buckskin dresses, and taught them the ways of their tribe.

Maske was the eldest sister. She was strong and wise, with a vivid imagination. The second sister, Elu, was shy and gentle like a delicate prairie flower. The third sister, Iha, was a fast runner and a skilled stickball player.

The fourth sister, Skata, loved to play games and tricks on everyone, including Maske. The fifth sister, Luta, was quiet and beautiful and was the first to greet the new day.

The sixth sister, Wisteca, was timid and shy and loved animals. The seventh sister, Mani, was the youngest. She loved making clothes and moccasins for her dolls from tree leaves. Maske and her sisters lived a happy life with their Até and Iná.

It was autumn, the season for harvest and preparation. Soon, Waziya, the old man of the north, would blow his white, icy breath across Maka. It would be a time for stories. Maske loved to tell her sisters stories about Mahpiya (Sky World), a magical place where stars scattered as far as the eye could see, like glittering stardust.

Maske and her sisters finished braiding tinpsila, the wild turnips Iná put in their buffalo stew, and hung them near the tipi door to dry. Iná wanted to make wojapi, a chokecherry pudding, but could not find her dried chokecherry patties.

Iná said, "Maske, please go to the edge of the village with your sisters and pick a small basket of cherries. Stay close together and do not wander too far away from the village."

It was well past the cherry gathering season, but Maske found a small chokecherry tree with a few black cherries. She tasted them.

"How sweet and ripe they are," she said.

After each sister also had a small taste, there were no cherries left to put in the basket.

Maske said, "We must go deeper into the forest. Perhaps we will find bigger trees."

They found a tree with twice as many cherries and started picking. The sisters enjoyed the warm sun on their backs and their visit with one another. Maske told her sisters about the boy in the next village with the long braids and big, kind eyes. She told them how she was bashful and hid from him when he looked everywhere for her.

Maske said, "I will be brave and talk to him at our next tribal gathering."

Maske's sisters giggled as they tried to imagine Maske, their brave sister, hiding in the bushes because she was too scared to talk to a boy. They laughed so hard they almost dropped their basket, unaware of the eyes that were watching them from the thicket.

A sound startled Maske and her sisters. It was the sound of a silent forest. No birds were chirping. No crickets were singing. There was just unusual stillness. Danger was in the air.

Elu said, "I am afraid. We have never been this far away from the village before. Let us return home now."

"Yes, we will go back to the village now," said Maske.

"G-R-R-R-R-R!"

The sound was deafening and sent chills through Maske and her sisters. An enormous shadow slipped through the trees. It was Mato Sica, the giant bear that loved to eat people.

aske shouted to her sisters, "Follow me, quickly! Run!"

They made it to a rock ledge, where they huddled together in fear. Mato Sica circled them, snorting and snarling, his long white fangs chomping with anticipation. Maske knew the short ledge offered them no defense.

She prayed to the Great Spirit: "Wakan Tanka, please help us and save us from the evil giant, Mato Sica."

A sudden jolt lifted up the ground beneath them. Maka began to violently shake and rumble. She swayed back and forth and rose higher and higher. Maske and her sisters remained huddled, their eyes closed tight.

Slowly, the fierce roar of Mato Sica faded into the distance. Although only a few minutes had passed before the earth's tremors finally stopped and the dust cleared, to the sisters it felt like an eternity.

Maske opened her eyes and looked around. They were standing on the top of a tall earth tower, high above the pines, high above the lakes and the rivers. Maske could see Mato Sica far below. Gnashing his teeth in anger, he clawed at each side of the earth tower. First he clawed the west side, then the north side, east side, and finally the south side, leaving deep gashes in the sheer walls from his sharp claws. Maske tried to be brave for her sisters, but she shuddered with fear.

Elu was the first to see it. "Look! In the sky! Something is coming toward us." Maske watched it soar closer and closer. It was a magnificent giant bird.

The bird announced his presence with a shrill, piercing cry. With a flutter of his wings and a great thud, he landed on top of the earth tower next to Maske and her sisters. Sitting next to Maske and her sisters was Wanbli Tanka, a huge sacred eagle. It was the largest bird Maske had ever seen.

Wanbli Tanka said, "Do not be afraid. I am your brother. I have come from Mahpiya to help you. Quickly climb upon my back and hold on tightly. I will carry you to safety."

Maske and her sisters climbed upon the back of Wanbli Tanka. They buried their fingers deep into his soft, warm tufts and held on tight. With a massive heave, he lifted, then rose higher and higher above the earth tower. He flew far above the black pines dotted with elk and buffalo, far above the rolling green hills painted with yellow and blue flowers, and far above the streams and blue lakes filled with ducks and beaver.

Far below, Mato Sica chased after them, following their path east toward the open plains. He ran faster and faster, panting harder and harder. With a final push, he dropped to the ground in exhaustion, leaving behind a cloud of dust. As he lay silent and still, he turned into a mountain of stone. Trapped forever in that moment, he would never again rain terror upon Maka.

Wind currents lashed and tore at Maske and her sisters as they soared far above Maka toward Mahpiya. Rising far above Hanwi (the moon) and far above Wi (the sun), they kept going higher and higher. Finally, they reached the land of Wicahpi (Star Nation).

A beautiful circle of tipis filled with tiyóspaye (family) welcomed them home. Maske knew Wakan Tanka had prepared a sacred place for her and her sisters in the Wicahpi.

That night, far below on Maka, the wind whispered to Até and Iná: "You must come to the edge of the village and look up. You will find us."

Até and Iná peered up into Hanhepi (the night sky). Their hearts filled with peace and understanding. They saw their daughters—Maske, Elu, Iha, Skata, Luta, Wisteca, and Mani—smiling down upon them. Seven brilliant stars, clustered together, shining like seven bright diamonds watching over them and all the people on Maka forever and ever.

To this day, the people are reminded of a time long ago in the "Heart of Everything," the Paha Sapa (Black Hills), when Mato Sica (Giant Bear) roamed Maka (Earth World) devouring everything in his path. A time when Wicincala Sakowin (Seven Sisters) cried out to the Wakan Tanka (Great Spirit) to save them from Mato Sica. A time when a tall earth tower rose up to save Wicincala Sakowin from Mato Sica. A time when Wanbli Tanka (Sacred Eagle) carried the Wicincala Sakowin to their new home among the Wicahpi (Star Nation).

Today, all that is left is the tall earth tower wearing the imprint of sharp claw marks, known as Mato Tipila (Bear Lodge). All that remains of Mato Sica is a rock silhouette named Mato Paha (Bear Mountain). And far above, in the night sky, resides Wicincala Sakowin, a promise to all that Wakan Tanka loves us and will always hear our prayers.

Bear Lodge
Mato Tipila

Bear Mountain
Mato Paha

Black Hills
Paha Sapa

Hinhan Kaga

Maka Oniye

Author's Note

ALFREDA BEARTRACK-ALGEO is a storyteller and poet as well as an artist and illustrator. She is a member of the Lower Brule Lakota Nation, Kul Wicasa Oyate, Lower Brule, South Dakota, where she grew up surrounded by her tiyóspaye, her circle of family and friends. Alfreda uses various art forms as a means to tell her stories. Alfreda says, "It is a very sensitive and beautiful experience to be a story-teller. There is a story in everything I create, from the smallest rock to the mightiest mountain. With every character born, every story shared, I add a piece of my spirit to this great matrix of life. As long as I have a story left to tell, I feel I have a responsibility to gift that story forward." Alfreda currently lives in beautiful Palisade, Colorado, with her spouse, David Algeo.

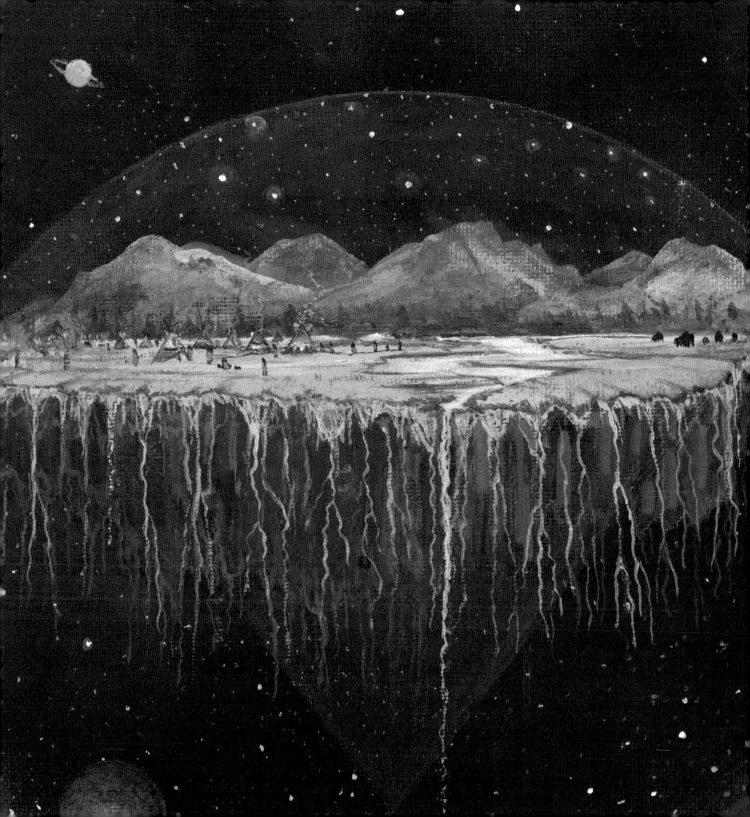